THIS
BOOK
BELONGS
TO

katie

DATE

The Books About Molly

★

MEET MOLLY · An American Girl
While her father is fighting in World War Two, Molly and her brother start their own war at home.

★

MOLLY LEARNS A LESSON · A School Story
Molly and her friends plan a secret project to help the war effort, and learn about allies and cooperation.

★

MOLLY'S SURPRISE · A Christmas Story
Molly makes plans for Christmas surprises, but she ends up being surprised herself.

★

HAPPY BIRTHDAY, MOLLY! · A Springtime Story
An English girl comes to stay with Molly, but she's not what Molly expects!

★

MOLLY SAVES THE DAY · A Summer Story
At summer camp, Molly has to pretend to be her friend's enemy and face her own fears, too.

★

CHANGES FOR MOLLY · A Winter Story
Dad will return from the war any day! Will he arrive in time to see the "grown up" Molly perform as Miss Victory?

MEET
MOLLY
AN AMERICAN GIRL

BY VALERIE TRIPP

ILLUSTRATIONS NICK BACKES

VIGNETTES KEITH SKEEN, RENÉE GRAEF

PLEASANT COMPANY

Published by Pleasant Company Publications
© Copyright 1986, 1989 by Pleasant Company
All rights reserved. No part of this book may be used or reproduced
in any manner whatsoever without written permission except in the
case of brief quotations embodied in critical articles and reviews.
For information, address: Book Editor,
Pleasant Company Publications,
8400 Fairway Place, P.O. Box 620998,
Middleton, WI 53562.

Printed in the United States of America.
99 00 01 02 03 WCV 37

The American Girls Collection® and Molly McIntire®
are registered trademarks of Pleasant Company.

PICTURE CREDITS
The following individuals and organizations have generously given
permission to reprint illustrations contained in "Looking Back":
pp. 54-55–The Bettmann Archive; Navy Department; The Bettmann
Archive; pp. 56-57–AP/Wide World, Courtesy LIFE Picture Service;
Library of Congress; D.O.D. Still Media Depository; Emma Hermann
Thieme; Kohler Co. Archives; © 1943 The Curtis Publishing Company;
pp. 58-59–Culver Pictures; L.L. Olds Seed Company; American Red
Cross; Alfred Eisenstaedt, LIFE Magazine © 1943 Time Inc.; Bulletin/
Temple Univ. Photojournalism Collection.

Edited by Jeanne Thieme
Designed by Myland McRevey

Library of Congress Cataloging-in-Publication Data

Tripp, Valerie, 1951–
Meet Molly: an American girl
by Valerie Tripp; illustrations, Nick Backes; vignettes, Keith Skeen, Renée Graef.

p.cm.–(The American girls collection)
Summary: While her father is away fighting in World War II,
Molly finds her life full of change as she eats terrible vegetables
from the victory garden and plans revenge on her brother
for ruining her Halloween.
[1. Brothers and sisters–Fiction. 2. Halloween–Fiction.
3. World War, 1939-1945–United States–Fiction.]
I. Backes, Nick, ill. II. Title. III. Series.
PZ7.T7363Me 1989   [Fic]–dc19   89-3907   CIP   AC
ISBN 0-937295-81-7   ISBN 0-937295-07-8 (pbk.)

TO MY FAMILY

TABLE OF CONTENTS

MOLLY
A nine-year-old who is growing up on the home front in America during World War Two.

DAD
Molly's father, a doctor who is somewhere in England, taking care of wounded soldiers.

MOM
Molly's mother, who holds the family together while Dad is away.

JILL
Molly's fourteen-year-old sister, who is always trying to act grown-up.

RICKY

Molly's twelve-year-old brother—a big pest.

BRAD

Molly's five-year-old brother—a little pest.

MRS. GILFORD

The housekeeper, who rules the roost when Mom is at work.

LINDA

One of Molly's best friends, a practical schemer.

SUSAN

Molly's other best friend, a cheerful dreamer.

CHAPTER ONE

TURNIPS

Molly McIntire sat at the kitchen table daydreaming about her Halloween costume. It would be a pink dress with a long, floaty skirt that would swirl when she turned and swish when she walked. There would be shiny silver stars on the skirt to match the stars in her crown. The top of the dress would be white. Maybe it would be made of fluffy angora, only Molly wasn't sure they had angora back in Cinderella's time. That's who Molly wanted to be for Halloween—Cinderella. All she had to do was

1. talk her mother into buying the material and making the costume,
2. find some glass slippers somewhere, and

3. convince Linda and Susan, her two best
   friends, to be the ugly stepsisters.

She could probably talk Susan into it. As long
as Susan got to wear a long dress, she wouldn't
mind being a stepsister. But Linda was another
story. If they were going to be fairy-tale princesses,
Linda would want to be Snow White because she
had black hair just like Snow White's. Linda would
want Molly and Susan to be dwarfs. *Probably Sleepy
and Grumpy,* thought Molly.

Well, Molly certainly felt like Grumpy tonight.
She looked at the clock. She had been sitting at the
kitchen table for exactly two hours, forty-six
minutes, and one, two, three seconds. She had been
sitting at the kitchen table, in fact, ever since six
o'clock when Mrs. Gilford, the housekeeper, called
everyone to supper.

Molly had smelled trouble as soon as she
walked into the kitchen. It was a heavy, hot smell,
kind of like the smell of dirty socks. She sat down
and saw the odd orange heap on her plate. She
made up her mind right away not to eat it. "What's
this orange stuff?" she asked.

Mrs. Gilford turned around and gave her what

2

Molly's father used to call the Gladys Gilford Glacial Glare. "Polite children do not refer to food as *stuff*," said Mrs. Gilford. "The vegetable which you are lucky enough to have on your plate is mashed turnip."

"I'd like to *re*turn it," whispered Molly's twelve-year-old brother Ricky.

"What was that, young man?" asked Mrs. Gilford sharply.

"I like to *eat* turnips," said Ricky, and he shoveled a forkful into his mouth. Eating turnips—or anything alive or dead—was no hardship for

Ricky. If it could be chewed, Ricky would eat it. Quick as a wink, all his turnips were gone.

That rat Ricky, thought Molly. She looked over at her older sister Jill. Jill was putting ladylike bites of turnip in her mouth and washing them down with long, quiet sips of water. Almost all of the horrible orange stuff was gone from her plate.

Molly sighed. In the old days, before Jill turned fourteen and got stuck-up, Molly used to be able to count on her to make a big fuss about things like turnips. But lately, Molly had to do it all herself. Jill was acting superior. This new grown-up Jill was a terrible disappointment to Molly. If that's what happened to you when you got to be fourteen, Molly would rather be nine forever.

The turnips sat on Molly's plate getting cold. They were turning into a solid lump that oozed water. With her fork, Molly carefully pushed her

meat and potatoes to a corner of her plate so that not a speck of turnip would touch them and ruin them. "Disgusting," she said softly.

4

"There will be no such language used at this table," said Mrs. Gilford. "Furthermore, anyone who fails to finish her turnips will have no dessert. Nor will she be allowed to leave the table until the turnips are gone."

That's why Molly was still at the kitchen table facing a plate of cold turnips at 8:46 P.M. *None of this would have happened if Dad were home,* she thought. Molly touched the heart-shaped locket she wore on a thin chain around her neck. She pulled it forward and opened it up to look at the tiny picture inside. Her father's face smiled back at her.

Molly's father was a doctor. When American soldiers started fighting in World War Two, Dr. McIntire joined the Army. Now he was somewhere in England, taking care of wounded and sick soldiers. He had been gone for seven months. Molly missed him every single minute of every single day, but especially at dinner time.

Before Dad left, before the war, Molly's family never ate supper in the kitchen. They ate dinner in the dining room. Before Dad left, back before the war, the whole family always had dinner together. They laughed and talked the whole time. Now things were different. Dad was gone, and every morning Molly's mother went off to work at the Red Cross headquarters. Very often she got home too late to have dinner with the family. And she spent at least an hour every night writing to Dad.

When a letter came from Dad, it was a surprise and a treat. Everyone gathered and listened in silence while Mrs. McIntire read the letter aloud. Dad always sent a special message to each member of the family. He told jokes and drew funny sketches of himself. But he didn't say which hospital he worked in or name any of the towns he visited. That wasn't allowed, because of the war. And even though Dad's letters were long and funny and wonderful, they still sounded as if they came from very far away. They were not at all like the words Dad spoke in his deep-down voice that you could feel rumbling inside you and filling up the house. Molly used to be able to hear that voice even when she was up in her room doing homework.

*Even though Dad's letters were long and funny and wonderful,
they still sounded as if they came from very far away.*

When Dad called out, "I'm home!" the house seemed more lively. Everyone, even Jill, would tumble down the stairs for a big hug. Then Dad would sit in his old plaid chair, cozy in a warm circle of lamplight, and they'd tell him what had gone on in school that day. Dad's pipe smoke made the room smell of vanilla and burning leaves. Sometimes, now that Dad was gone to the war, Molly would climb into the plaid chair and sniff it because that vanilla pipe smell made her feel so safe and happy, just as if Dad were home.

Molly remembered the fun they had at the dinner table when Dad was home. He teased Jill and made her blush. He swapped jokes with Ricky and told riddles to Brad, Molly's younger brother. And he always said, "Gosh and golly, olly Molly, what have *you* done today?" Suddenly, everything Molly had done—whether it was winning a running race or losing a multiplication bee—was interesting and important, wonderful or not so bad after all.

Dad loved to tease Mrs. Gilford, too. As she carried steaming trays out from the kitchen with lots of importance, Dad would say, "Mrs. Gladys Gilford, an advancement has been made tonight in the art of cooking. Never before in the history of mankind has there been such a perfect pot roast." Mrs. Gilford would beam and bustle and serve up more perfect pot roast and mashed potatoes and gravy. She never, ever, served anything awful like turnips.

But everything was different now because of the war. Dad was gone and Mom was busy. So Mrs. Gilford, who had arrived at the dot of seven

o'clock every weekday morning of Molly's life to cook and clean, now ruled the roost more than ever. And Mrs. Gilford was doing her part to help win the war.

A Victory garden was Mrs. Gilford's latest war effort. Last spring she sent away for a pamphlet called *Food Fights for Freedom*. It explained how to start a Victory garden in your own backyard. The pamphlet had a picture of vegetables lined up in front of a potato and an onion that were wearing military hats and saluting. Under the picture it said "Call vegetables into service."

"From now on, there will be no more canned

vegetables used in this house," Mrs. Gilford announced. "The soldiers need the tin in those cans more than we do. From now on, we will grow, preserve, and eat our own vegetables. It's the least we can do for our fighting boys."

All summer long, Mrs. Gilford had tended her Victory garden. She wore a stiff straw hat, Dr. McIntire's gardening gloves, and knee-high black rubber boots. Everyone, even little Brad, had helped her. Molly had worked in the Victory garden every Tuesday morning from ten to eleven o'clock. She had crawled on her hands and knees through rows of green seedlings, pulling weeds. The rows were as strict and straight as soldiers on parade. Each one was labeled with a colorful seed packet

Call
VEGETABLES
INTO SERVICE

on a stake. The seed packets showed fat carrots, plump red tomatoes, and big green peas.

But by fall, after months in the hot sun, the pictures on the seed packets had faded away. The packets hung on the stakes like limp white flags of surrender. Mrs. Gilford's Victory garden had not been quite as victorious as she had hoped. All but the toughest vegetables had been beaten by the dry summer. The carrots were thin and wrinkled. The tomatoes were hard as nuts. The peas were brown. But that did not defeat Mrs. Gilford. Mrs. Gilford would never give up and open a tin can. She had a rather successful crop of radishes, lima beans, and turnips, so that's what they would eat.

As Molly stared at the turnips on her plate, she remembered Mrs. Gilford saying, "Wasting food is not only childish and selfish, it is unpatriotic. Think of your poor father off in some strange land. Maybe he didn't have enough to eat tonight. And you turn up your nose at fresh turnips. You will not leave this table until those turnips are gone. Completely."

Now it was almost nine o'clock. It was getting cold in the kitchen. Molly was lonely. She was tired of thinking about how unpatriotic she was. She looked at the turnips, lifted a tiny forkful, and put it in her mouth. Just then Ricky burst through the swinging kitchen door.

"How do you like eating old, cold, moldy brains?" he teased. Then he ran out.

Molly swallowed the turnips fast, then gulped down a whole glass of water. Old, cold, moldy brains was exactly what the turnips were like. She would not eat one speck more.

"Ricky, you rat!" she said. "I'm going to get you!" She started to get up from the chair.

From behind the door Ricky chanted, "Nyah, nyah, nyah-nyah nyah! You can't leave the table. You haven't finished your turnips!"

"Ricky, stop it!" yelled Molly. But Ricky was right. The turnips were still on her plate and she was stuck. To make matters worse, Molly heard her mother calling good-bye to the car pool she rode with from Red Cross headquarters.

Now Mom will be mad at me, too, thought Molly. *Now she'll never make a Cinderella dress for my Halloween costume. Now everyone in the house will be mad at me for making Mom upset. And all because of these terrible turnips.*

Mrs. McIntire walked in the back door, looked at Molly, looked at the plate, and knew immediately what had happened. "Well, Molly," she said. "I see we had the first turnips from the Victory garden for dinner tonight."

"Mom," said Molly, "I hate turnips. I know I do. And Mrs. Gilford says I can't leave the table until I eat them. I'll be here until I die, because I will never eat these. Never. I really mean it."

"I see," said Molly's mother. "Do you mind if I join you for a while? Not until you die, of course—just while I have a cup of tea. And while I'm heating up the stove, why don't I reheat those turnips for you? They certainly don't look very good when they're cold like that."

"It won't help," said Molly.

But Mrs. McIntire scooped up the turnips and put them in a frying pan. "I'll just smooth out these lumps. And I think we can spare a little bit of our sugar and butter rations to add to the turnips," she said, almost to herself. "And a little cinnamon, too."

Soon a delicious, spicy aroma filled the kitchen. The kettle whistled, and Mrs. McIntire made her tea. She spooned the turnips back onto Molly's plate and put the plate in front of Molly.

The hot steam from the turnips warmed Molly's face and clouded her glasses. She took a deep breath, raised a small forkful to her lips, and tasted it. It wasn't so bad. In fact, it was pretty good— sweet, cinnamony, and kind of like applesauce.

It felt good going down, not at all like old, cold, moldy brains. She ate another forkful.

Mrs. McIntire sat down with her tea. "When I was about your age," she said, "my mother made sardines on toast for dinner one night. Little oily dead fish on toast! I refused to eat them. But my mother said I could not leave the table until the sardines were gone. *Gone* was exactly what she said. So when she wasn't looking I put each sardine, one by one, into my napkin. Then I stuck my napkin into my pocket. When my mother saw my empty plate she was surprised, but she excused me from the table.

"I used to play checkers with my father every night after dinner. That night it was very hard to concentrate on the game. Our two cats, Bessy and May, yowled and meowed and climbed all over me. They smelled the sardines. Finally, when I had one hand on Bessy and the other hand on a checker, May pulled the napkin out of my pocket. The sardines spilled out all over the rug. Bessy and May gobbled them up."

"Oh, Mom!" laughed Molly.

"Oh, Molly," sighed Mrs. McIntire. "Sometimes

14

*"The war has changed things," said Mrs. McIntire.
"But some things are still the same."*

we have to do things whether we like it or not. There aren't always cats around who will eat the sardines." She reached across the table and brushed Molly's bangs out of her eyes. "I know this war is hard on you children. And I know you miss your father. I miss him, too."

"Everything is so different with Dad gone," said Molly. "Nothing is the way it used to be anymore."

"The war *has* changed things," said Mrs. McIntire. "But some things are still the same. Isn't Ricky still Ricky?"

"He sure is," said Molly. "Still dumb old Ricky."

"And you are still my olly Molly," said Mrs. McIntire. "And I am still me." She gave Molly's hand a squeeze.

Molly smiled. The turnips were gone. Mom was not mad. Mrs. Gilford wouldn't think that Molly was ruining her war effort.

"Thanks, Mom," she said as she gave her mother a hug. She walked carefully up the stairs to bed, pretending she was wearing a long, floaty pink skirt that swished as she took each step.

HULA
DANCERS

The next morning dawned all gold and blue and windy. *Perfect Halloween weather,* Molly thought as she woke up. At breakfast Mrs. Gilford didn't say anything about the turnips, but she made French toast, which was a sign that all was forgiven.

It was Thursday, and Molly's friends Linda and Susan were coming home with her after school. They were going to plan their Halloween costumes. They had made a secret pact not to discuss their ideas until they got to Molly's house. "Someone might copy us if they heard our idea," said Molly. Linda and Susan agreed. Besides, it was fun to have a secret pact—it was sort of like being soldiers and keeping battle plans away from enemy spies.

As they walked home after school they met Alison Hargate, who was one of their classmates. She asked, "What are you three going to be for Halloween?"

"We can't tell," said Molly. "It's a surprise."

"Oh," said Alison.

Linda said, "But it's *great*. It's really a great idea."

Susan chimed in, "Yes! It's wonderful! We're going to have the best Halloween costumes ever."

Alison looked impressed. Molly was a little worried. The girls hadn't even agreed on what they were going to be. The mystery was making their costumes get a lot of attention. They were really going to have to make good costumes, or else everyone would tease them.

"What are you going to be, Alison?" Molly asked.

"Oh, probably an angel," said Alison. "My mother said I could wear her white satin dressing gown, and she's already made me some gold wings and a halo."

Molly, Linda, and Susan were suddenly very

quiet. Molly was jealous. She was sorry she had even asked Alison. An angel! What a great idea! Alison was sure to look wonderful with a halo over her golden hair.

It was very hard to have Alison for a friend. Alison was an only child, and her parents were rich and gave her everything that anyone could want. Alison didn't mean to brag about the things she had, but just by telling the truth she managed to make everyone resent her.

"My mother doesn't even have a dressing gown, much less a white satin one," said Linda glumly. "All she has is a brown terry cloth bathrobe. I know she'd never even let me wear that."

DRESSING GOWN

"Well," said Molly to Alison, "all I can tell you is that *our* idea is much more . . . um . . . original than an angel."

"Yeah, I know an angel is kind of boring," said Alison quickly. "It was my mother's idea. She made the wings and all."

"Well, see you later, Alison," said Molly as she and Linda and Susan hurried away. It made them uncomfortable when Alison started being so *nice.*

When the girls got to Molly's house, they went into the kitchen for a snack.

"Hello, Mrs. Gilford," they said together.

"Hello, girls," answered Mrs. Gilford. She was watering the parsley plants she'd started to grow on the kitchen windowsill. "There are some apples in the bowl on the table. Help yourselves, but take your apples outside, please. It's too nice a day to be cooped up in the house."

"Thank you, Mrs. Gilford," the girls said as they

went to sit on the back steps in the sunshine. Ricky was out back, too, shooting baskets at the hoop on the side of the garage. He was trying to set a world record for making the most baskets without missing.

As the girls munched their apples, Susan said, "Gee, I think an angel is a good idea. Why don't we be angels, too?"

"Absolutely not," said Molly. "Do you want Alison to think we stole her idea?"

"Alison wouldn't mind," said Susan.

"I know," said Molly. "But *I* would mind. We can think of something just as good."

"Like what?" asked Linda.

"Well," replied Molly slowly, as if she had just thought of it for the very first time. "How about Cinderella and the two ug— I mean, the two stepsisters?"

"Oooooh," said Susan. "Cinderella!"

"Who gets to be Cinderella?" Linda asked immediately.

"We don't have to decide that right away," said Molly. "Let's . . . uh . . . let's wait and see who has the best ball dress, and that's the one who will be Cinderella. The other two will be stepsisters."

"I don't think it's fair," Linda stated. "Who wants to be an ugly stepsister?"

"You're all ugly step *sitters* today," teased Ricky. "Get it?"

"Cut it out, Ricky," said Molly. Ricky went back to shooting baskets.

"I think it's a good idea," said Susan. "My sister Gloria just gave me an old prom dress of hers. It's sort of green, with a big petticoat and shiny gold threads at the bottom of the skirt. I'll wear that."

"Sort of green," Ricky mocked. "Lima bean green is what you mean."

"Ricky, go away," said Molly. But she was thinking that Susan's dress sounded perfect for Cinderella. And it had two very big advantages over Molly's floaty pink dress with the white angora top. Susan's dress really existed, and Susan already had it. Being an ugly stepsister was not at all what Molly had in mind.

"Wait a minute," she said. "Maybe Linda is right. Maybe it's not fair. Maybe we should all be exactly the same thing, like the Three Musketeers."

"You'd be perfect as the Three Little Pigs," said Ricky. "Or you could be the Three Bears. How about the Three Stooges? Or the Three Kings of Orient?" He began to sing in a loud, teasing voice:

"We three kings of Orient are,

Tried to smoke a rubber cigar,

It was loaded, it exploded . . ."

"STOP IT!" yelled Molly.

And suddenly, Ricky did stop. His face turned red. He bounced the basketball under his legs, then behind his back. He leaned casually against the garage and twirled the ball on the tip of one finger.

The girls turned around to see who he was showing off for. It wasn't Mrs. Gilford or even Mrs. McIntire. Nobody was there except Jill and her new best friend Dolores. They were walking up the driveway, carrying their school books.

Dolores was wearing a bright blue sweater just the color of her eyes. She had a wide, white smile,

like a movie star in a toothpaste ad. She stopped and flashed her smile at Ricky.

23

"Hi, Rich," she said.

"Rich!" snorted Molly. Lately, Ricky had been telling everybody to call him Rich because it sounded more like a soldier's name than Ricky did.

"Hi, Dolores," he squeaked in a very odd voice. He turned quickly, jumped, and sent the basketball swishing through the basket just as Dolores went in the door.

Molly, Linda, and Susan looked at each other and dissolved into giggles. It was crystal clear to them what Ricky's problem was. Ricky-Rich had a crush on Dolores! The three girls started to chant:

"Ricky and Dolores up in a tree,
K-I-S-S-I-N-G!
First comes love,
Then comes marriage,
Then comes Ricky with a baby carriage!"

Ricky threw the basketball at the girls. But they hopped up and out of the way, making loud, slurpy kissing noises. "Ricky has a crush!" they chanted. "Ricky loves Dolores!"

"Hi-i-i, Do-lor-esss," Molly squeaked, imitating Ricky. She pretended to kiss the basketball.

"Eeeeeuuuuwwww!" Linda and Susan shrieked.

"You'll be sorry!
You'll pay for this!" Ricky called.

Ricky jumped on his bike. As he sped past the girls he called, "You'll be sorry! You'll *pay* for this!"

The girls just giggled until they ran out of breath and their stomachs hurt. Finally, they got serious again and went back to the question of what to be for Halloween.

"We could be the princesses of England," suggested Linda.

"There are only two of them, Elizabeth and Margaret Rose. One of us would have to be their mother," said Molly.

"How about being nurses?" asked Susan. "We could all wear capes."

"That's what we did *last* year!" Linda and Molly said together.

They considered being acrobats, three Alices in Wonderland, ice skating stars like Sonja Henie, or the Three Blind Mice. No one could get very excited about being a blind mouse, and anyway, Mrs. McIntire overheard them and said she absolutely did not have time to make a mouse costume for Molly. "And besides," added Mrs. McIntire, "in wartime I don't think it's right to use good material for Halloween costumes."

26

Molly, Linda, and Susan groaned. They knew Mrs. McIntire was right.

"But I've got another idea, girls," said Mrs. McIntire. "I'll show you how to make grass skirts out of newspaper and crepe paper. Then you can be hula dancers."

"Well," replied Susan, "my sister Gloria taught me how to make flowers out of crepe paper, just like they did to decorate for the prom. We could string them together and make flower necklaces and headdresses."

"I think my father has an old ukulele," said Linda. "It doesn't have any strings, but it will look good."

"It's too bad it's so cold, because I know my mother will make me wear socks and shoes and a sweater on top," said Susan. "But at least the flower necklaces will hide most of the sweater."

So the girls decided to be Hawaiian hula dancers for Halloween.

Soon after that the street lights went on, which meant Linda and Susan had to go home. They agreed to meet back at Molly's house after school the next afternoon, to make their costumes. Then they would all go trick-or-treating together. Afterwards, Linda and Susan would spend the night at Molly's so they could talk about how wonderful their Halloween had been.

By the time she went inside to supper, Molly had completely forgotten Ricky's threat to make them all sorry. She was too busy practicing her hula.

TRICK
OR TREAT?

The grass skirt made out of newspaper and crepe paper was not exactly as glamorous as the pink floaty skirt Molly had imagined. But it was quite long, and it did make a nice rustling noise as she walked. Besides, making the skirts had been lots of fun. Mom came home from Red Cross headquarters early, just so she could help. She put on a record of Hawaiian songs. Then they all sat in the den, cutting the newspaper into strips. They covered the newspaper with strips of green crepe paper. Mom sewed all the paper onto long pieces of cloth to tie around their waists like aprons. Susan showed them how to make crepe paper flowers that were big and colorful.

They made strings of the paper flowers to use as necklaces and bracelets. Mrs. McIntire even squirted some of her perfume on them.

By the time they were ready to go out trick-or-treating, Molly, Linda, and Susan were caught up in the excitement of Halloween and very pleased with their matching hula outfits.

"Adorable! You look as cute as buttons!" said Dolores. She and Jill bobby-pinned the big flowers into the girls' hair.

"When I get back from taking Brad trick-or-treating, I'll take your picture to send to Dad," said

Mrs. McIntire. Brad was wearing a sheet. He was going as a ghost. "Ricky, I'll want a picture of you, too."

"Okay, Mom," said Ricky. He was dressed as a pirate. Ricky was a pirate every year.

It was a windy night, but not too cold, so the girls rolled down their socks and pushed up the sleeves of their sweaters. The wind made their skirts ripple so that they looked graceful and pretty, just like real grass skirts.

They saw Alison when they went to the Silvano's house down the street. Her angel outfit was perfect. She had a flowing white satin robe with fluffy white feathers at the neck and cuffs and all down the front. Her wings and halo were covered with gold glitter.

"Hula dancers!" Alison sighed with envy when she saw them.

Molly was very pleased. *They* had made Alison jealous. "Your outfit is good, too," Molly said. "You really look like an angel." She felt like being nice. In fact, it would probably be fun to trick-or-treat with Alison, except Alison's mother always went with her.

"Hawaiian hula dancers!" Mrs. Hargate was saying. "What charming costumes, gals! And homemade, too! Aren't you clever?" The girls just smiled and hurried away.

"Really," Linda said later, "you almost have to feel sorry for Alison with a mother like that!"

"I know," said Molly. "Wouldn't it be awful to have a mother who doesn't know that the whole *point* of Halloween is to go out and walk around the neighborhood with your friends, and not with her?"

Because of the war, most people did not have any sugar to spare, so the girls did not get as many candies and cookies as last year. Nevertheless, their brown paper bags were soon bulging with apples, doughnuts, molasses kisses, peanuts, and popcorn balls. The Hargates' maid was giving out Tootsie Roll Pops, which were the best treats.

Two families, the Pedersons and the Rucksteins, asked the girls to do a trick before they got their treats. So the girls did a hula, waving their arms and singing the Hawaiian song they learned in school. Linda

strummed her stringless ukulele. It was
a big hit. The Pedersons, especially,
clapped and clapped. They gave the
girls each two glasses of cider.

Linda believed in eating her treats along the
way, so her bag was not as full as Susan's and
Molly's when the girls finally walked back up the
driveway to Molly's house. Molly was humming the
Hawaiian song, Linda was unwrapping a popcorn
ball, and Susan was making her skirt swish and
sway. They were almost to the back door when a
huge splash of water poured down on top of them
and a hose sprayed straight at them.

"AHHHH!" Molly yelled. The water flooded
around her feet in cold gushes. She felt as if she
was drowning in a waterfall. Her bag of treats
burst, the popcorn balls floated in puddles, the
doughnuts turned to spongy globs, the apples rolled
away down the sidewalk. Linda and Susan were
gasping. Their paper flowers were flattened. Their
skirts were hanging in shreds. The green dye from
the crepe paper was dripping down their legs onto
their socks.

When the water finally stopped, Molly's hair

*A huge splash of water poured down on top of them
and a hose sprayed straight at them.*

34

was stuck to her forehead, her hands were full of melting paper flowers, and most of her hula skirt lay in soggy ribbons in the driveway.

"Ruined! Wrecked! Completely wrecked!" sobbed Molly. "Who would play such a mean trick?"

Then the girls heard Ricky singing in a low, slow, steady voice:

"I see London,

I see France,

I can see your underpants!"

"Ricky," yowled Molly, "I'll get you for this! You ruined everything! You'll be sorry—you wait! You'll be *really* sorry."

Ricky threw the hose down and ran off. The girls just stood there in the driveway, stunned with surprise and sputtering with anger. Maybe they shouldn't have teased Ricky about Dolores, but who ever would have expected him to get back at them in such a terrible, mean way?

Finally Linda said, "I'm freezing!"

Molly said, "You two go on inside. I'll clean up this mess. Then we've got some planning to do. We have to teach Ricky a lesson he'll never forget."

CHAPTER
FOUR
—

WAR!

A while later, Linda, Susan, and Molly sat in Molly's room in their pajamas. Still pink and warm from their baths, wrapped head to toe in big white blankets, they looked like three rosy polar bears. The girls were whispering together on Molly's bed when they heard Mrs. McIntire returning with Brad.

"Would you hula dancers like some cocoa?" Mrs. McIntire called up to the girls.

"Okay, Mom," called Molly. "We'll be right down."

"Good!" said Susan. "Now we can tell her what Ricky did!"

"No!" Molly said quickly.

36

"Why not?" asked Susan.

"I don't want to be a tattletale," said Molly. "Besides, she'd be too easy on him. We have to take care of Ricky ourselves."

The girls walked slowly into the kitchen. There at the table sat Ricky, still in his pirate costume. He was sipping cocoa and looking as innocent as a kitten. Molly, Linda, and Susan sat as far away from Ricky as possible.

"Well, girls," said Mrs. McIntire. "How was your Hawaiian Halloween?"

"Fine," said the three girls all together, but it sounded as if they meant just the opposite.

Mrs. McIntire looked puzzled. "Just 'fine'? That's all?" she asked. "And why are you all in your pajamas already? I wanted to take your picture to send to Dad. What happened to your costumes? And your bags of treats?"

"They got wet," said Molly.

"Wet?" asked Mrs. McIntire. "How?"

The girls looked at each other. "By a hose," said Susan. "Ricky—"

"We walked into a hose. By mistake," said Molly quickly, before Susan could finish.

"Who would be using a hose on a windy Halloween night?" asked Mrs. McIntire.

The girls said nothing. Finally Molly said, "Just someone."

Mrs. McIntire frowned. "Molly McIntire," she said. "I have the distinct feeling that I am not being told the whole story."

Molly stared into her cocoa cup. Ricky pushed his chair back from the table.

"Perhaps *you* can tell me what happened, Ricky," said Mrs. McIntire.

"Me?" squeaked Ricky. He fiddled with the handle of his pirate dagger. "I didn't . . . I mean . . . I mean . . ."

"Go on, Ricky," said Mrs. McIntire.

"Well, it was just a joke, Mom," said Ricky. "Just a joke on the girls. You know, a Halloween joke? Trick or treat?"

"A *mean* trick," muttered Linda.

"What did you do?" asked Mrs. McIntire, staring steadily at Ricky.

"I just got a little water on their costumes," said Ricky.

"A *little* water?" squealed Molly. "You dumped

"Perhaps you can tell me what happened, Ricky,"
said Mrs. McIntire.

pails and pails of water all over us, Ricky!"

"You squirted us with a *hose!*" Susan added indignantly.

"You ruined our costumes and all our treats!" said Linda.

"Is that true?" asked Mrs. McIntire.

"Yes!" exclaimed all the girls.

"Ricky?"

"Yes, ma'am," muttered Ricky. He looked at his feet.

Mrs. McIntire was quiet. Then she said, "Ricky, that was a very mean thing to do. I'm ashamed of you, treating your sister and her friends that way. I think I can say that your father would be ashamed of you, too. I'm going to punish you just as I think he would have punished you." Mrs. McIntire sighed. "You are to apologize to these girls. Then you are to give your bag of Halloween treats to Linda, Susan, and Molly to share. You may keep one treat, and only one, for yourself. I'm going upstairs to put Brad to bed now, and while I'm gone I want you to apologize. Is that clear?"

"Yes, ma'am," said Ricky.

"Girls, after Ricky apologizes, I want you to go

to bed. I'll come in later to say good night," said Mrs. McIntire as she left with Brad.

After she had gone, Ricky muttered, "Sorry." Then he shoved his bag of Halloween treats into Molly's hand and ran out of the kitchen.

As the girls trudged up to bed, Linda whispered, "You were right, Molly. She was way too easy on him."

"Yeah!" said Susan. "Except for the part about your father being ashamed."

"He wrecked our Halloween, and he's hardly suffering at all!" added Linda.

"Well," said Molly as she flopped on her bed, "we'll just have to think up a plan to make Ricky *really* suffer."

"Let's let the air out of his bicycle tires," suggested Susan.

"Not bad enough," said Molly.

"We could put frogs under his pillow," said Linda. "Dozens and dozens of frogs."

"Yeah, but then we'd have to catch the frogs," Susan pointed out.

"Eeeeeuuuuwwww!" they all shrieked.

"We could disguise our voices and call him up on the telephone," said Susan. "We could pretend we're Mrs. Mobley, his teacher, and say he has to stay after school every day next week for being bad."

"No," said Molly. "That's no good. It doesn't embarrass him in front of anybody. We have to really embarrass him in front of lots of people, or in front of someone he'd hate to be embarrassed in front of, like Mom, or . . ."

"Or Dolores!" said Linda.

"Yes, that's it!" said Molly. "Embarrass him in front of Dolores!"

"But how?" asked Susan.

The girls were quiet for a minute. Molly was still mad—as mad as a wet hen, her father would say. She could remember Ricky chanting,

"I see London,

I see France,

I can see your underpants."

Underpants? Dolores? Molly thought. Then she smiled to herself.

"I think I have a plan," she said to Linda and

Susan, "but all three of us have to cooperate or it won't work."

The next morning was Saturday. The breakfast table was crowded. Dolores, who had spent the night with Jill, was talking about the movie they were all going to see that afternoon. Ricky came to the table last. His hair was slicked back with water. *That's probably so Dolores will notice him,* thought Molly, but she didn't say anything. She wouldn't say anything to Ricky—she was still too mad about what he had done the night before.

Susan was the first to start the plan to get back at Ricky. She asked Mrs. McIntire for three big brown bags. "We need them to hold our Halloween treats," she said with a look at Ricky. Mrs. McIntire gave her the bags.

Linda had a harder job to do. She had to keep Ricky out of his room for a while after breakfast. "Can I watch you shoot baskets?" she asked Ricky. "I want to learn how."

"Girls can't play basketball," answered Ricky rudely.

"Ricky!" said Mrs. McIntire. "What an unfriendly thing to say! You march outside like a

gentleman and show Linda how to shoot baskets.
She is our guest."

"Yes, ma'am," said Ricky.

He and Linda went outside. Mrs. McIntire
walked with Brad to the mailbox around the corner
to mail a letter to Dad. Dolores followed Jill up to
her room to listen to records.

As soon as Jill's door closed, Molly and Susan
dashed into Ricky's room. They flung open the top
drawer of his dresser and dumped his underwear
into a brown bag. They turned his laundry bag
upside down on the floor, gathered the underwear
and dirty socks from the pile, and stuffed them into
the other two bags. They made one last
quick check to be sure the room did not
look disturbed before they rushed back
to Molly's room.

The window in Molly's room
looked out over the back door and
driveway, where Ricky was shooting baskets and
Linda was watching. Molly opened the window
wide. "Okay, go on," she whispered to Susan.

"I can't do it," hissed Susan. "I'm too scared.
And it's lying."

44

"Go *on*, Susan," said Molly. "You *have* to do it. Linda and I will never speak to you again if you don't. Just cross your fingers, then it's not a lie."

"Okay," said Susan. She went and knocked softly on Jill's door. Jill and Dolores were inside practicing the rhumba.

"What do *you* want?" Jill asked Susan.

"Well," said Susan, "I thought you'd like to know that Russ Campbell is at the corner in his car. He told me to run in here and tell you two—I mean *ask* you—if you wanted to go for a ride with him."

"Russ Campbell?" Jill and Dolores shrieked. Russ Campbell was the senior football star at Montgomery High School, where Jill and Dolores were freshmen. A ride in Russ Campbell's car was a dream come true for them.

"Oh, how do I look?" asked Jill in a panic.

"You look fine," said Dolores. "Gosh, I'm glad we curled our hair last night!"

"Let's go!" said Jill. "Let's go before Russ changes his mind."

"Okay!" said Dolores. The girls galloped down the stairs, but just before they went out the back door they slowed down, patted their hair, smoothed their skirts, and straightened their shoulders.

Susan ran back to Molly's room. "Get ready! They're on their way outside!"

Seconds later, just as Dolores and Jill strolled out the back door, Molly and Susan leaned way out the window, yelled as loud as they could, and turned the big brown bags upside down. Underwear and T-shirts filled the air like giant, floppy snowflakes. Dozens of socks tumbled down. A T-shirt got caught in the basketball hoop. A dirty sock landed on Jill's shoulder. Some plaid under-shorts landed right on Dolores' head.

"What's *this?*" asked Dolores in disgust as she lifted the underwear off her head with the very tips of her fingers.

Molly, Susan, and Linda chanted:
> "I see London,
> I see France,
> Those are Ricky's underpants!"

*Underwear and T-shirts filled the air
like giant, floppy snowflakes.*

47

 "RICKY!" screeched Jill. "That's REVOLTING!" She threw the dirty sock at Ricky. "And I suppose that business about Russ Campbell was part of the joke, too! Of all the stupid, *childish* things to do!"

"But I *didn't*," Ricky wailed.

"Here, Ricky," Dolores interrupted. She was still dangling the undershorts from her fingertips. "I believe these cute little underpants belong to you, don't they?" As she tossed them to Ricky, she winked at Jill. Suddenly, they both started to laugh. They laughed so hard they had to sit down on the back steps and laugh some more. Ricky got very red in the face. He ran around frantically collecting his socks and underwear.

Finally Dolores gasped, "Come on, Jill. Let's go to my house. At least we can be pretty sure we won't be showered with some little kid's underwear!" Jill and Dolores started down the driveway, still laughing at Ricky.

Molly called out the window, "There's YOUR Halloween trick or treat, Ricky!"

48

"I'll get you!" Ricky yelled back. "You'll be sorry! This is *war!* This is really war! I'll—"

Suddenly Ricky stopped. He stood still in the driveway. Jill and Dolores stopped, too.

Molly and Susan leaned out of the window to see why. There was Mrs. McIntire, standing at the end of the driveway with Brad. Her face was as hard and cold and white as a marble statue. "Uh-oh," said Susan. She slid down to the floor next to Molly.

Mrs. McIntire looked up at the window. "Come down here at once, girls," she said sternly. "Jill and Dolores, I want you to hear this, too."

In seconds, everyone stood on the back steps. Molly's legs were shaky. No one said anything. Then Mrs. McIntire began to speak.

"Until there are no more tricks in this house, there will be no more treats," said Mrs. McIntire. "Instead of going to the movies, Ricky, you will spend your day raking the yard. Make sure you rake up the Halloween mess you made—all the bits of costumes, all the ruined food. Susan, Linda, and Molly, you will spend your day doing Ricky's laundry. I want everything washed, hung out to dry, folded, and put away by the end of the afternoon. Jill and Dolores, you will take care of Brad."

Mrs. McIntire paused. She looked straight at Molly, then straight at Ricky. "I suppose these tricks you have been playing on each other don't seem very serious to you. But they are mean, childish, and wasteful. I'm disappointed in you, but more than that, I'm sad and discouraged. If we can't get along together, who can?"

Molly looked at Ricky. Ricky looked at his mother. "This fighting *has* to stop," Mrs. McIntire went on. "This is exactly what starts wars—this meanness, anger, and revenge. Two sides decide to get even and end up hurting each other. There's war and fighting enough in the world, and I won't have any more of it in our house. Is that understood?"

Everyone mumbled, "Yes, ma'am."

"All right, then," said Mrs. McIntire. "Get to work." She went inside.

Molly stood up and faced Ricky. "Give me your un—uh, your things," she said.

"Here," said Ricky. "I think that's all of them." He pushed the bundle into her arms.

50

"Okay," said Molly. "Listen, we didn't—I
mean, we didn't want to keep fighting with you,
exactly. We were just mad. We wanted to embarrass
you. We shouldn't have done it. I'm sorry. I really
am."

"It's okay," said Ricky. "I guess I deserved it."
He began to smile a little. "Your trick was mean,
but you know, it was funny, too." He laughed. "I'm
kind of glad not to be fighting against you any
more. You three have pretty good ideas, even if you
are a bunch of triple dips. I guess it's better to be
on your side than to be your enemy."

Molly grinned. "Thanks, Ricky," she said. She and Linda and Susan went inside.

It wasn't so bad doing Ricky's laundry. Molly, Linda, and Susan pretended they were three Cinderellas *before* the ball. So, in a way, Molly got to be Cinderella for Halloween after all. And later, when the girls went outside to hang the laundry on the clothesline, Mrs. McIntire came out to help them.

"It sort of looks like an underwear tree, doesn't it?" she said when they were finished. She smiled down at Molly, who turned and gave her a hug. Her mother was right: it was much better not to be fighting.

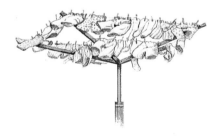

LOOKING
BACK
1944

A PEEK INTO
THE PAST

AMERICA
IN
1944

If you lived in Molly's world you probably would have had a big radio in your living room. You'd listen to it for fun, just like you watch television today. You'd wait to hear each new episode of *The Green Hornet*. You'd listen for the train whistle on *I Love a Mystery*. And your whole family would probably try to answer "The $64 Question." Many families like Molly's were listening to the radio on December 7, 1941, when they heard the announcer say:

> We interrupt this program to bring you a special news bulletin. This morning, Japanese planes attacked the American military base in Pearl Harbor.

Many American soldiers and sailors were killed in the bombing of Pearl Harbor. People all over the United States were angry and wanted to fight back. They felt the faraway war they'd been hearing about for the last two years wasn't so far away anymore.

World War Two had begun long before December 7, 1941. In Europe, the German army had already attacked peaceful countries like England and France. Germany's leader was a dictator named Adolf Hitler. Hitler and his followers, the Nazis, wanted to stretch their power until they controlled the world. After Pearl Harbor was bombed, Americans joined the war to stop the Germans and the Japanese.

Adolf Hitler

Thousands of American men volunteered to fight. They became soldiers, pilots, and sailors. They drove ambulances and tanks. They worked as doctors, mechanics, and cooks. Women joined the armed forces, too. They worked in military hospitals and offices. They drove jeeps, ordered supplies, and nursed the wounded.

Men and women served their country.

Almost every family in the United States had to say good-bye to someone who went to war. People missed their relatives, just like Molly's family missed Dad. But they were also proud of these men and women. To show their pride and love, people hung blue stars in their windows, one for each family member who was away at war. If someone was killed, the family hung a gold star in the window.

People worried about their relatives who had gone away to war. Like Molly and her family, they wondered where the people they loved were and whether they were safe. Soldiers

Censored letter

American factories made war equipment.

could write letters to their families, but they weren't allowed to say much about what they were doing. And their letters were *censored*—parts of them were cut out—so that enemy spies could not read them and learn where Americans were ready to fight.

When American soldiers joined the fighting, American factories "went to war," too. Car factories made airplanes and tanks instead of new cars. Clothing factories made uniforms and tents instead of dresses. Shoe factories made boots for marching instead of shoes for playing. Factories that once made toys were changed to make war equipment.

Before the war, most American women did not have jobs. But as men went away to fight, more and more women went to work in offices and factories.

Rosie the Riveter

They built and tested airplanes, repaired train engines, and ran businesses. Women proved they could do any job that needed to be done.

Even people who did not go off to fight said they were "fighting on the *home front*." People on the home front changed the way they lived so that the United States could win the war. They drove their cars less so there would be plenty of gas for airplanes, tanks, and army trucks. They stopped buying food in cans so the metal could be used for guns and bullets instead. They raised their own food by planting Victory gardens so that the food farmers grew could go to the soldiers.

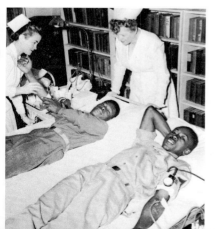

Americans helped the Red Cross by giving blood.

58

A "blue star mother" waits for her son.

People working on the home front often volunteered to do important work without pay. They knitted socks, made bandages, and packed boxes of food to send to the soldiers. Some worked for the Red Cross, like Molly's mother did, collecting blood to help wounded soldiers.

World War Two was hard for people who fought and for people on the home front. Millions of people were killed. Many more were wounded. Americans who stayed at home were often frightened and lonely, but they were also proud of what their country was doing. They were willing to make the sacrifices they did because they believed that if they could win the war, the world would be a better place for everyone.

THE AMERICAN GIRLS COLLECTION®

FELICITY   JOSEFINA   KIRSTEN   ADDY   SAMANTHA   MOLLY

Did you enjoy this book? There are lots more! Read the entire series of books in The American Girls Collection.® Share all the adventures of Felicity, Josefina, Kirsten, Addy, Samantha, and Molly!

And while books are the heart of The American Girls Collection, they are only the beginning. Our lovable dolls and their beautiful clothes and accessories make the stories in The American Girls Collection come alive.

To learn more, fill out this postcard and mail it to American Girl, or call **1-800-845-0005**. We'll send you a catalogue full of books, dolls, dresses, and other delights for girls.

I'm an American girl who loves to get mail. Please send me a catalogue of The American Girls Collection®:

My name is _____

My address is _____

City _____ State _____ Zip _____
1961

My birth date is ___ / ___ / ___
          Month Day Year

Parent's signature _____

And send a catalogue to my friend:

My friend's name is _____

Address _____

City _____ State _____ Zip _____
1225

If the postcard has already
been removed from this book
and you would like to receive
an American Girl catalogue,
please send your name and
address to:

AMERICAN GIRL
PO BOX 620497
MIDDLETON WI 53562-9940
Or call our toll-free number:
1-800-845-0005